MY GR

ALSO BY JAN HERMAN

General Municipal Election: A Multimedia Rant
Cut Up or Shut Up (co-author)
Something Else Yearbook (editor)
Brion Gysin Let the Mice In (editor)
A Talent for Trouble: The Life
of the Hollywood Director William Wyler
Second Nights
Ticket to New Jersey
My Adventures in Fugitive Literature
Collateral Damage: The Daily History of a Blog
Erato: The Writer's Curse
Fragments
The Z Collection

―――

Chapbooks of Deformed Sonnets:
Fourteen; Mortal Coil; Small Thefts;
Mistress Death; Songes (Dreams);
The Way the Lines Break; Shitstorm

―――

Your Obituary Is Waiting
All That Would Ever After Not Be Said
Kleine Tiere (Small Animals)
Shadow Words

MY GRUB STREET

Jan Herman

*"Grub Street is a metaphor
evoking the eternal spirit
of the hack writer."*
—Philip Pinkus

PHANTOM OUTLAW EDITIONS

Copyright © 2023 by Jan Herman. All rights reserved.

Book design by Jakob Boyarsky.

The first four tales in this modest collection were published in translation in the German magazines *LUI* and *TransAtlantik* in 1986 and 1987. They have not appeared in the original English until now. The facts and figures in all seven tales reflect the period in which they were published. Except for purposes of a published review this book, or parts thereof, may not be reproduced, stored in a retrieval system, or transmitted in any form by any means, including mechanical, electronic, photocopying, recording, internet, or otherwise, without written consent of the author or publisher.

Contents

Bad Boy 7

Brothel 13

Scams 25

Underworld 41

Exit From Fleet Street 55

The Professional 63

His South Africa 69

Author Note 74

Bad Boy

AT HIS GLASS-WALLED MANSION on a California mountain top overlooking Monterey Bay, the perpetual bad boy of Borland International was having trouble being good. His corporate advisers had counseled him in recent months to sanitize his style. They wanted him to adopt the manner of a pinstriped executive. He should not only stop shooting off his mouth, he should be punctual and, at the very least, quit wearing those loud Hawaiian shirts.

So here it was almost midnight and the guests he had invited home to dinner at 10 o'clock that evening were still waiting for him to show up. Nobody was surprised. Philippe Kahn had not become an overnight millionaire in computer software by being punctual. Or conventional. And when he finally did arrive, explaining without apology that he had decided to polish up his tennis for a few hours on the spanking new court behind his office, he regaled his guests throughout dinner with anecdotes that would have made his corporate advisers cringe.

The 37-year-old former mathematics teacher with a bear-like girth, a head of thick black hair, a puckish face, and a brash sense of humor, recalled the time he withdrew one million dollars from his company's bank account and had it delivered to his office in hundred-dollar bills because — unaccountably — he had been refused a credit card. "I was just fed up," he said over dessert at nearly one in the morning. "They kept telling me I had no credit references. So I told them to have the money brought to my office the next morning in brown paper bags because I was going shopping. They said, 'That's a funny joke.' I told them it was no joke."

A past master of outrageous pranks, Kahn said he showed up at his office in an undershirt because he guessed — correctly — that the bank officials accompanying the delivery would be dressed in three-piece suits. "The biggest luxury in life is being able to say *scheisse* to your banker," Kahn declared.

Not to mention, a life filled with some conspicuous luxuries that would be hard to top:

• Two ocean-going sailboats, a 43-foot Finnish-built Baltic racer (the "Dolphin Dancer") and a 70-foot California-made sloop (the "Katmandu").

• A couple of Porsches sitting unused in the garage because the police had caught him doing 130 mph in a 55 mph speed zone and had his driver's license suspended.

• An all-terrain Suzuki Samurai to tool around the forty steeply wooded acres of his 'Hawk Hill' estate.

• A recording studio and four pianos to noodle on (including two in his bedroom) when he is not playing the saxophone, or the flute, guitar, or congas.

• Another recording studio off the courtyard with a heated swimming pool and spa, where he can watch the clouds roll in at eye level from the Pacific.

"I didn't want to get rich," Kahn insisted. "I just wanted to make a decent living for my family and a few friends. I came to the States on a tourist visa to look for work in Silicon Valley. But nobody would give me a job because I didn't have a green card. Without it, I wasn't allowed to work."

When he purposely overstayed his tourist visa, which made him an illegal alien, Kahn decided to start his own business. "I figured I could blend in, and the authorities wouldn't know where to find me."

Of German-Jewish extraction, Kahn was born and reared in Paris. His parents separated during his childhood. His father was a businessman. His mother, who worked in the movie industry, was a survivor of both Auschwitz and Buchenwald. She died when Kahn was 13 years old. "I was on my own after that," he recalled. "My father was in Paris. But he let me stay in my mother's apartment with a housekeeper as long as I kept up my grades. Nobody told me what to do. I was pretty happy."

Kahn took up karate (earning a black belt), studied English at the UNESCO school, went on to the Eidgenossische Technische Hoch Schule in Zurich (where he studied computer science for three years), then got a master's degree in mathematics at the University of Nice, in France.

By 1982, after spending a year living like a hermit in the Pyrenees — he tended a flock of sheep — Kahn began his computer software company at home in an apartment above a supermarket.

Ironically, getting orders for his software programs was easier than cashing them. Kahn took the orders on credit-card slips borrowed from a restaurant. But when he brought the slips to the bank, it refused to honor them.

"They didn't want my business." Kahn recounted. "They said there was too much mail-order fraud. We battled for weeks to cash those slips. They wouldn't do it until a friend put up his house as collateral."

Today, Borland International occupies two vast building in Scotts Valley. It is the sixth-largest software company in the United States with annual sales of $62 million (in fiscal 1986) on a wide array of products: Sidekick, Paradox, Quattro, Sprint, and others. As chief executive officer and the major stockholder, Kahn owns approximately 66 million shares. His holdings are worth about $26.6 million at current market prices. He also controls more than fifty percent of the voting stock.

With success like that, Kahn could not exactly "blend in." Nor did he try. A marketing genius with a flair for the unorthodox in business, he made news with his increasingly flamboyant personal gestures. He was fond of throwing toga parties, for instance, and playing impromptu saxophone solos at company press conferences. It wasn't long before the American immigration authorities caught up with him.

"I don't really know how they found me," Kahn insisted. "But I believe I was turned in by some of my competitors."

After he was tossed out of the U.S., in 1985, it took a battery of lawyers to smooth his return along with his wife, Martina, and their teenage daughters, Laura and Estelle.

"You know," Kahn said. "I always hear how I threw these famous toga parties. But I never hear anybody talk about the one really big party that screwed up a deal worth $75 million. That story is never told now. And it's much more fun."

Kahn grinned. It seems that in 1985, not very long after Borland shipped its first product, McGraw-Hill (a billion-dollar publishing corporation) decided to explore a possible purchase of Kahn's company. "They asked me to come to New York," Kahn said. "I had never been there. I didn't even own a tie. I get to the Time-Life building and I'm brought up to the McGraw-Hill boardroom. The conference table was as long as a battleship. And there's a row of faces and I'm thinking to myself, 'Uh. shit. They look like wallpaper.'

"They asked questions. I answered them. Next day more meetings. They audit the company and they make an offer: $75 million. Not bad. People in the company who had stock said. 'Let's make it happen.' I was torn," Kahn said. "You build a company and you're just going to give it away? It's not that they're going to break it, like a toy or something. It's just that you believe in it. And you can't just start another company. They make you sign one of these 'non-compete' clauses, which means the only thing you can do is go into the fruit-juice business.

"But I finally said, 'Okay.' The board of McGraw-Hill approves the deal. The next day I get a call at seven in the morning. It wakes me up. 'Philippe, have you read the papers?' I said, 'No, I never read the papers.' They said. 'Well, you're on the front page of the Wall Street Journal and it says you threw a drunken orgy and all you had to say about it was, 'I can't quarrel with the drunken part. I only wish I remembered the orgy.' On top of that it says you're an illegal alien!' I think one or the other might have been okay, but not both."

His face beamed. He looked like an imp, a florid 265-pound imp. Far from being disappointed that the deal fell through, Kahn said, he was actually pleased. Had it been consummated he would have had to move to Manhattan to run Borland for several years as part of the deal. And that would have driven him crazy.

"City life is not for me," he said. "I like the way things are in California. I like nature. I like living on a mountain. I lived for 18 years in the city. Paris. I know every street corner. When I go back, it's amusing for two or three days. But that's enough. Here I have the woods and the ocean. And I can go sailing whenever I want."

The Dolphin Dancer, which he bought two years ago for $259,000, is only minutes away at a dock in Santa Cruz. Kahn is, in fact, a very serious sailor. Two years ago he won the four-and-a-half-day Cabo San Lucas race (from

Los Angeles to the tip of Baja California in Mexico) with Dolphin Dancer. Last year he won the 10-day Pacific Cup race (from San Francisco to Hawaii) at the helm of the Katmandu, which he charters by the year and keeps in Honolulu. Now he is contemplating a month-long, three-man race from Hawaii to Hiroshima, also on the Katmandu. The race commences in June. Eventually he hopes to make a solo trans-Pacific crossing.

"Ocean racing is always an adventure," said Kahn. "I'm interested in self-reliance. These days I'm practicing single-handed. I have fun at whatever I do. But I'm also serious. I like to do things well."

Indeed. It is precisely the raffish independence which Kahn's straightlaced corporate advisers want him to suppress that seems indispensable to his drive for achievement. "I love sailing and I'm very good at it," he reflected. "But you can't make a living by sailing. So I translate my sense of mastery and adventure, which some people call flamboyance and unpredictability, from sailing to computer software. Simple, no?"

Simple, yes. Like a latter-day buccaneer, Kahn has even been known to hold Borland directors' meetings aboard the Dolphin Dancer when the mood strikes him. "Why not?" he asked. "If you can't have fun, what's the point?"

LUI, 1987

BROTHEL

EVEN IN AN ERA of sexual revolution, when roles are changing radically, the age-old battle of the sexes rages on unchanging. As Gay Talese put it in *Thy Neighbor's Wife*, women are still selling and men are still buying.

It may be subversive to resurrect the old D. H. Lawrence notion that the male libido virtually has a will of its own with no particular loyalties, indeed with a compelling need for endless variety. But for "working girls" who make their living in Manhattan's many brothels, that notion is proved time and again by daily experience and tidy profits.

Consider Hannah, a tall, attractive, first-year medical student at the most prestigious university in New York. Hannah leads a double life studying by day and turning tricks by night. For the past eight months she has worked in a middle-class brothel on the Upper West Side, where she earns $1,000 a week on average for three shifts a week. Straight sex with Hannah — which can include "French," "69," and kissing — costs $150 per hour, or $80 per half-hour. Extras, like spanking, "Greek," or "Around the World," cost an additional $30.

"There's so much moralizing about working in a house that I don't go around telling people about it," says the raven-haired doctor-to-be. "But I'm not ashamed of it. My clients like the pleasure I give them and I'm perfectly clear about what I'm doing and why I'm doing it. It pays for my education, which isn't cheap, and gives me time to study. I knew I wouldn't be able to get by on student loans or waitressing. When you actually become a working girl, it's not that big a deal."

Working girls, she explains, often turn tricks as a sideline — sometimes for a few months, sometimes for a few years. Being "in the life," as she says, is a way to stake yourself to the career you really want. A friend of hers is paying for law school with her brothel earnings. Another recently launched a successful clothing business. Many working girls come from the art world, having migrated to New York from the best colleges with ambitions of becoming painters. It doesn't take them long to discover that menial jobs like art gallery receptionist won't pay the rent, but sex-for-hire will.

Unlike veteran streetwalkers "on the stroll" along the avenues or homeless teenage hookers who hang out along the Deuce (their term for 42nd Street), these middle-class courtesans tend to be mostly in their 20s, well-mannered, well-dressed, and highly articulate. Like Hannah, they can blend in so well at a fashionable cocktail party that only a practiced eye could tag them for hookers. Picking them out of a crowd of Broadway theatergoers would be next to impossible.

"You're supposed to look conservative but available somehow," says Hannah, sipping tea on the sofa of an artist girlfriend's downtown loft. "There is a rule of thumb that all the girls use: Dress as if you've just had lunch with your mother and you're on your way to see your boyfriend's parents."

Hannah herself is tastefully outfitted in a gray knit suit, a white blouse, heels, and stockings. She is wearing large but simple gold earrings. Her eyes are made up with only a hint of eye shadow, and her lips are glossed with blushing pink lipstick. She looks, in a phrase, refined yet alluring.

"For the men who come to a house, it's almost an addiction," Hannah says, smiling. "They really can't stay away. After you work for a while, you realize how many men can't communicate with the people in their lives — at home or at the office. In a brothel they can achieve a certain intimacy, bizarre as that sounds. They can have a secret life and act out their fantasies. What's really strange is that they don't have any other outlet for this."

Smart, capable, ambitious, and — paradoxically — feminist, Hannah points out a considerable irony: all the Victorian parlor manners that women once learned to win a husband in an earlier century — how to be polite, how to make conversation — are now put to use in the brothel trade, where clients want the illusion of a romantic "date." Still, it takes more than a little humoring to keep up a semblance of romance with a client like Doctor Dan.

"Dan can't get excited until I beg him to cure me of a disease," Hannah recounts with a laugh. "The first time I laid eyes on him I thought he'd want missionary-style sex. But you can't always predict these things. He's big and balding, with a mustache and a little weenie. Well, he put his weenie between my fingers, like it was some kind of Havana cigar. So I thought, he doesn't want it missionary style. He wants me to smoke it. Or maybe all he really wants is a sloppy hand job."

Dan, who turned out to be a middle-aged corporate lawyer with a wife and two daughters, has become one of

Hannah's regulars. Except for needing her to pretend she's paralyzed until he "cures" her, she says, Dan seems otherwise normal. He makes a salary in six figures as a partner in a law firm. He has a house in the suburbs. He goes hunting in the woods during the fall and deep-sea fishing off Bermuda in the spring.

"He really surprised me," Hannah says. "How can I give him a hand job if my hands and fingers — my whole body — is supposed to be paralyzed? That's when I find out he can only get a hard-on if I tell him I've got this condition and I've already been to a specialist and the specialist can't cure me. So what I need — Oh, please, Doctor Dan! — is a medical miracle. As soon as I say those words — "medical miracle" — his prick stands up like a flagpole. He's been back four times now and I've been cured of polio, arthritis, multiple sclerosis, and myasthenia gravis. The diseases keep getting more exotic. If he keeps coming back, I'm going to run out of them."

Amused though she is, Hannah can't help wondering why so many American men have peculiar erotic fantasies. "I know this country has a Puritan hangover," she says, "but you'd think we'd have gotten over it by now."

Historically, zealots like Anthony Comstock, who once turned New York into a battleground for the suppression of sex, are to blame. America's sexual hang-ups, typified by a hypocritical attitude toward prostitution, might have been different had Comstock not come along. A vengeful, 19th-century evangelist who makes Jerry Falwell of the Moral Majority look like a timid Sunday school preacher, Comstock tried to stamp out vice with his marauding "purification campaigns."

In addition to the anti-sex laws he inspired in 1873, some of which are still on the books, this self-described "weeder in God's garden" gained the legal power of arrest at the peak of his career and managed to herd hundreds of "sinners" into various prisons. He also entrapped scores of prostitutes, ultimately causing the suicides of 15 women who could not face the humiliation of a public trial for immorality.

Comstock, who secretly recorded in his diary the excessive shame he felt for being an obsessive masturbator, thus forged a direct link between the church and the vice squad. Today, while the linkage has become indirect, the moral regulators and censors still fervently attempt to inspire private sexual guilt. Perhaps that is what Doctor Dan is "curing" when he plays out his weird fantasy. Indeed, because there's so much "theater" in the brothel trade, Hannah says she's grateful for her undergraduate training as an actress before she decided to become a doctor.

"I took a circuitous route to medical school," says Hannah, 30, who was born and reared in Brooklyn and graduated from New York University in 1979 as a drama student. "I was a good enough actress to get some roles in Off-Broadway plays. But I soon realized I'd have to get work outside of the theater to support my acting ambitions. So I decided to acquire a nursing degree."

Academically first-rate through college — "I never got anything less than 'A' in any of my courses" — she also was a top student in her nursing classes. By then, however, she had become more interested in science than theater. Coincidentally, two of her nursing professors took her aside and advised her that she was too bright for nursing. She should become a doctor. Accordingly, she decided to switch careers and went back to college to take all the biology and chemistry courses needed for medical school.

In the meantime, it was in one of her nursing classes that Hannah met Debbie, now a medical nutrition researcher, who gave Hannah the idea of earning her med-school tuition by working in a brothel. Debbie had been a working girl herself on and off for years.

They had gone for a drink one evening after class and got to talking about the illuminating contradictions of life in New York. And that's when Debbie revealed that she supported herself by hooking, suggesting that Hannah might give it a try if she ever needed money for school.

Debbie, 32, a vivacious redhead who still speaks with a faint Southern accent, comes from a wealthy Georgia family. She is shorter than Hannah and curvier in her stylish hip-hugging mini-skirt and sleeveless tank top. Childhood ballet lessons gave her beautiful legs. And the spike heels Debbie is fond of wearing accentuate the curve of her calves. Although she has not worked in a brothel on a steady basis for some time, she still occasionally turns tricks on weekends for extra money.

"I got into the life because my father refused to let me go off to college," Debbie says, sitting opposite Hannah on the edge of a large coffee table. "He wouldn't pay for my education. We lived in a small town. He wanted me to marry his business associate's son. It was an arranged marriage. That just wasn't what I wanted. When I refused, he threatened to cut me off.

"So I decided to get out. I came north and had a few jobs. Then I answered an ad for what I thought was a receptionist's job. It turned out to be for a brothel 'hostess' on the East Side. I believed I could handle it. I worked at that house for six months and learned the trade."

One of the many things Debbie learned was that freckle-faced redheads with pert noses and pale blue eyes were not in great demand even if they'd been Prom Queen back home. "You'd think a Georgia peach would have been some kind of exotic attraction," she says. "But men just don't go crazy for redheads. I've got nice big tits, though, which they do like. That balanced my checkbook. I'll tell you, working in a house you learn a lot about stereotyping."

For instance, in a typical Manhattan brothel catering to a clientele of businessmen who stop by at lunchtime or during the cocktail hour, the madam always tries to have certain types of girls on duty: a blond, a brunette, an Asian, a college girl, and a light-skinned black. Says Debbie: "The house manager — that's what madams prefer to be called — also wants someone there with big tits. That's really important. And she doesn't want any dark-skinned women or Hispanic women or any women who don't speak English well."

In fact, skin color, education, social class are all sold as commodities. Educated white girls bring higher prices than high-school dropouts or light-skinned blacks. Indeed, for a black girl to work alongside white girls she must either be especially beautiful or even better dressed than the madam. And generally the black girl is kept around only because a small but predictable portion of the white clients want her type. So when somebody calls up to make an appointment, he'll hear the madam tick off the merchandise like a head waiter offering chef's specials: "Today we have a college girl, a beautiful blond, a buxom brunette . . . "

Far from being brutalized by pimps, today's working girls are more likely to be badgered to death by a yuppie madam who is smarmy enough to qualify as a boutique proprietor. Says Hannah: "The madam where I'm working is so extremely well dressed I think she must spend her life shopping."

Generally the style of the brothel will reflect the neighborhood it's in. If a man is seeking a place with refined, upscale women, he will more likely find them at a brothel in a high-rise apartment on the Upper East or Upper West Side than in a less desirable neighborhood. If he can't afford the sort of rates Hannah and Debbie charge, he may patronize the cheaper midtown brothels near the United Nations.

Yet one of the inescapable facts of Manhattan prostitution — 90 percent of which occurs indoors and not on the street — is that the women at any of the brothels are frequently interchangeable except for those at the really downscale houses.

"I would say that the girls pretend to be different, but they're all basically the same," says Debbie, who claims to have worked off and on at two dozen houses since she was 19 years old. "They create the illusion that you're getting more for your money by their style of dress or by the amount of pampering they give you. Everybody thinks the women who work for escort services are so deluxe. Many go back and forth between brothels and escort. A lot of the girls in the brothels won't work escort, and vice versa."

The reasons apparently have very little to do with beauty or class, but rather with temperament, money, and hours. Debbie "worked escort" when she was between houses. She was asked to stay on but didn't like the irregular schedule it required. "I found it easier to work in a house," she says. "A lot of girls feel that way."

Still, there are differences. "The girls in a brothel are more cut and dried," Hannah says. "They'd rather not be bothered with niceties. When they pamper a client, it's only because of the house style. They wouldn't spend as much time with a client if they didn't have to. Whereas girls who work escort like the chance it gives them to go to a fancy hotel or eat at a fine restaurant. To them it's a perk. They like the pretensions of working escort — getting picked up by a limousine, meeting people from all over the world. It helps some of them justify what they're doing, which is really no different than doing it in a house."

Surprisingly, many women actually prefer employment in a cheap, downscale brothel. "They can make the most money there in the least time," Debbie says. When she first started out at an upscale place — it was a two-room apartment in Greenwich Village with only two girls per shift — Debbie's fee came to $100 an hour or $70 for the half. She had to split everything down the middle with the madam, including whatever she made for "extras." The tips customers volunteered also had to be split with the house. Plus she had to pay a cleaning fee of $5 per "date," which adds up to a considerable amount when you're averaging a dozen sessions per shift.

Debbie says she made more money at "an abominable place near the U.N., where the girls sat around in negligées and the apartment was so falling-down funky it looked like a taxi dispatcher's office." The lower prices ($70 an hour, $40 the half) brought in much greater volume. More important, the house didn't care what happened in the bedroom so long as it got its half of the basic fee. The girl might make less for straight sex, but anything else she earned during the session was hers to keep. And the house didn't set a rate schedule for "extras." She could charge what she wanted.

"In the nicer houses, management wants a split on everything," Debbie points out. "On top of that, the girl has less control of what goes on in the room because she has more rules to follow. I averaged about $1,000 a week in the fancy places and $1,500 in the lousy ones. I put most of that away. It paid for school, and I lived pretty well. I got my bachelor's degree in biochemistry at Rutgers University and a master's degree in nutrition.

"I'm still in touch with my family," she continues. "But you know what? My father doesn't care that I've got two degrees. It bothers him. I think it would bother him less if I told him how I paid for them."

Both women say they have minimized their fear of AIDS by practicing "safe sex" — that is, never without a condom. "I'd say the men who come to a house are more frightened of AIDS than we are," Hannah volunteers. "But I don't think they can stay away. Not the regulars. Their fantasies are too compelling."

Like Hannah, Debbie dismisses the idea that there's anything shameful in being a working girl. "It's strictly economics," she insists. "Do you know any other kind of work the average woman can do to make $400 a day? I guess the only time I ever felt humiliated was when I had to put on that negligée and sit around all might like a cheap whore."

Of course, more elegant settings than a midtown whorehouse are no insurance against humiliation. Debbie recalls that "the worst session I ever had in all the days I ever had" happened in a posh brothel on Sutton Place, which ranks among New York's more exclusive addresses. She remembers the client as "the vibrating asshole."

"This man walked in with an Armani suit on," she recounts. "Beautiful shoes, beautiful watch. His hair was cut just right. He swept in like an ocean liner and picked me out. I was delighted. I poured him a scotch. It was going like clockwork. But once we got into the bedroom, he was cruel. He wanted so many fringes it was abusive. I felt like I was being raped. I mean, I did things for him I wouldn't do for my boyfriend. I finally had to stick a vibrator up his ass to bring him off. And then he wanted to thank me by pissing on my tits. It was a total power play. The man was vile. He didn't even offer a tip."

Debbie says she gradually got to know the men who came to that house more intimately than working girls usually get to know their tricks. "They gave me their real names," she says. "I knew their jobs. I knew where their wives shopped. They showed me pictures of their kids. And I found out that men in high positions can be the creepiest. Their thing is power, not sex. Why do they need to be so creepy? I've never been able to figure it out."

Debbie's story about "the vibrating asshole" reminded Hannah of the time she took a call from a customer who turned out to be a lesbian wanting to see two girls putting on a show. "She even offered to bring her own vibrator," Hannah says, amused. "Some houses will allow women customers in, but very rarely." Furthermore, the myth that prostitutes are basically lesbians and don't truly enjoy sex with men is just that — a myth.

"There are no more lesbians in brothels than anywhere else," Hannah says. "I've done some shows with other girls — some guys really get turned on by that — but it doesn't turn me on. Most of the working girls I've met like fucking men."

Nevertheless, one of the paradoxes of the trade is the working girl's reaction to sex in her own love life. Many prostitutes desperately need a boyfriend if only to remind themselves that "there's a difference between having sex for money and having it for real," Hannah observes. Her own reaction is very much the opposite.

"I'd rather not be touched, but I'm too busy to have a boyfriend now anyway," she says. "Even if I weren't, I wouldn't want to be with somebody who found it okay for me to spend a few days a week fucking strangers. Intellectually, you can say it's fine, that it makes no difference. But I don't think anybody can handle it emotionally. Besides, I wouldn't want to be with somebody who *could* handle it. That's a very alienated person."

Debbie more or less agrees. She had a boyfriend while working full-time and didn't tell him she was turning tricks. "Living a lie was really difficult," she says. "When I finally did tell him, he was afraid I enjoyed it. He couldn't conceive of my doing it for the money.

"We had this argument. I told him I didn't feel it. He said, 'How can you not feel it?' Of course you feel it physically. But not emotionally. Maybe that's why women have been able to do this for centuries. If you don't have that ability to detach yourself, you can't work."

TRANSATLANTIK, 1987

SCAMS

AT THE MANHATTAN Detention Center, better known as the Tombs, John Homer stared at the ceiling. He was awaiting arraignment for larceny. "I shoulda never went two hundred. I go a hundred and the dad gets on his plane and flies back to Chicago."

Stale smoke from the cigarette he was smoking curled through the air. His lantern-jawed face had the ashen pallor of a junk-sick junkie. At 27, he looked as used up as the stepped-on cigarette butts that had collected beneath his shoe. "Now I'm facing a year back on Rikers," he said.

Lt. John Kelly, a former narcotics cop who commands the Special Frauds Squad of the New York City Police Department, agreed. "He's probably right about the year." Kelly was sitting several streets away in his office on the 11th floor of 1 Police Plaza, the NYPD headquarters. "But he's wrong about Chicago. The victim came from Minneapolis."

According to Kelly, New York is unmatched in the breadth and variety of its scam artists, from ordinary pickpockets to "crying kids," from "pigeon drop" cons to "handkerchief switchers," from "three-card monte" dealers to fraudulent "bank examiners."

John Homer specialized in the "drunk with the gold coin" con. As he told it, he'd been running the scam on Manhattan's West Side for 10 days in a row. He knew that was a risk. If the bunko squad got a flurry of complaints making a pattern, it would send two plainclothes cops onto the street after him.

But he and his partner Joe Delaney needed $250 a day just to stay straight. There was no way to ease up.

Homer had not slept in a bed of his own since getting out of Rikers three months earlier. He sometimes paid five bucks a night for a windowless cell enclosed in chicken-coop wire at a Bowery flophouse grandly named The Palace Hotel. He could have gone to one of the free municipal men's shelters, but they were open dormitories unsafe at any price. Some guys went to sleep in a shelter and night prowlers made sure they never woke up. Having protection was worth five bucks.

On the afternoon that led to his arrest, a bleakly overcast Friday, Homer had already got the brush-off three times. It was his own fault. He should have been more careful picking his targets. The last one had nearly panicked when he made his approach. He knew as soon as he tugged her sleeve that he shouldn't have. Moms were right for pickpockets, wrong for the coin scam. This one almost called a cop.

Fuming at himself, Homer had retreated to Seventh Avenue and West 53rd Street. There he came to a halt and posted himself in front of a liquor store as the noontime crowd poured by. His choice of location might have seemed spontaneous but was in fact premeditated. The way he and Delaney worked the coin scam they wanted a public phone booth as close to Homer's approach as possible, and there were two phone booths on the corner.

Homer spotted a target within moments. Bearded, well dressed in a camel-hair overcoat and felt-brimmed hat, the target carried a suede attaché case and an umbrella. Although the sidewalks were dry, he also had on a pair of rubbers. Homer was tickled. The perfect dad, he assured himself. Square as they come.

When the target reached the corner, Homer materialized at his elbow. "C-c-can you help me, m-mister?" The man turned and saw a tall, plaintive figure with stringy hair and watery blue eyes, offering an envelope. His stammer was so pronounced that he was difficult to understand. Taken by surprise, the man hesitated and leaned closer. A Good Samaritan.

"I c-can't read this," Homer said, rooting the man to the spot with what seemed a palsied gesture. "I f-found it in the g-gutter." He offered the envelope for closer inspection. It came from the vault department of Manufacturers Hanover Trust, or so it seemed. In handwritten letters, the name of a Dr. James Stone was neatly printed above a 1065 Park Avenue address, along with a telephone number. The Good Samaritan bent to read it.

"I f-found these in the env-v-vel-l-lope," Homer added, leaning on the stammer and pulling from his pocket four old U.S. coins packaged in fresh cellophane-and-cardboard wrappers. "M-mayb-b-be I c-could get a reward to g-give them b-back." His voice was beseeching. "W-will you help me d-d-dial this number, huh m-mister?" Then he threw in some foot-shuffling, a pathetic hippety-hop.

It wasn't long before the Good Samaritan was turning the coins over in his own hands. Astonished, he could see the collector values carefully noted on each wrapper: an 1884 Liberty nickel ($365); a 1979 Large Cent penny ($1,565); an 1893 Barber dime ($635); an 1859 Indian Head penny ($715). They were real coins. Homer had bought them from a coin dealer for a grand total of $2.90, wrappers included. He could get a virtually unlimited supply of coins. All he had to do was write in the values.

The Good Samaritan, by now led to the public phone booth, dialed in the belief that he was doing the right thing. Apparently, Dr. Stone was a numismatist and had obviously lost the coins. The target was reassured of this when the doctor came on the line. "You must have seen my advertisement in the newspaper." The doctor was amazed and gratified that his offer of a reward for the lost coins had brought such immediate results. "What luck!" The reward was $750, he said.

No, the Good Samaritan hadn't seen the ad. He hadn't even found the coins. But it was good to know there was a reward because the gentleman standing next to him who *had* found the coins looked like he could use the reward money. Homer inexplicably would not take the phone. "Is he a street person?" the doctor asked, his tone suddenly anxious. Told that, yes, this gentleman appeared to be destitute and perhaps drunk, the doctor said, "You must secure those coins for me, sir. Have they been damaged? Are they in wrappers? They're extremely valuable."

The Good Samaritan was now caught in a crossfire. Homer muttered that all he wanted was a drink. If there was no reward, the hell with the coins. He'd go panhandle. He glowered. He took the coins from his pocket, where he had put them "for safe-k-keeping," he said, and looked at them with surly contempt. He'd sell the coins to someone. He wanted a bottle and a room. The doctor, meanwhile, beat a tattoo of worried words into the phone asking that Homer not be let out of sight until the coins were "secured."

In the end, the Good Samaritan succumbed to the irresistible urge of virtue masked by cupidity. He peeled $200 from his billfold at Homer's wheedling insistence and took a cab to 1065 Park Avenue to collect the reward himself — and was absolutely dumbfounded to discover there was no Dr. Stone. The doorman told him that five other people had turned up the day before asking for the same doctor.

Wounded, then miffed, the Good Samaritan took another cab to police headquarters, where he picked Homer's face out of a photo file. He was the fourth victim to do so in a week. One of Kelly's men dutifully took down the Good Samaritan's story, and Homer was arrested several days later.

Lt. Kelly, thickening into middle age, had commanded the Special Fraud Squad for the past two years. The view from his office window looked out over City Hall and beyond to the Twin Towers of the World Trade Center. They loomed above the steep canyons of Wall Street's financial district. It was an especially appropriate view considering the historic fraud of the Ivan Boesky case, which had lately rocked the city government and the stock market. But if Kelly's quarry consisted mostly of small-time cheats not comparable to political grafters in high places or the inside traders who were expected to be convicted, there were more than enough petty scammers to go around. They could fill a stadium.

"Right now we have photos of 10,000 individuals that we consider to be active on the streets of this city," Kelly told me. "And we are updating our photo file all the time." Ten thousand scammers working the streets? It was mind-boggling. "That's what we believe," Kelly insisted. Ironically, John Homer, despite his subsistence-level survival, was a rare breed of scammer. Among the 10,000, Kelly knew of only four con men who were actively running the coin scam.

Street scams have been a way of life in New York City for a very long time. A hundred years ago, before Damon Runyon glorified its hustlers, there were phony horse traders operating out of elegant downtown stables selling so-called "thoroughbreds" that dropped dead as soon as they hit the street. "Sawdust men" made the rounds of neighborhood taverns carrying bags of "real" money they were able to sell at discount because, as the story went, the bills had been printed on stolen government plates.

Nowadays days stolen electronic goods by the boxload pop up on so many Manhattan streets that they seem like legitimate warehouse sales: radios, stereos, tape decks, headsets, computers, alarm clocks, televisions. Hawkers of bogus brand-name watches and worthless gold chains are streetcorner fixtures. "Check it out, my man! Check it out!"

Then there are the old-time swindles, the clever cons that require ruthless artistry, the street scams grounded in basic criminal psychology, the sort that exploits the sympathy, gullibility, or greed of "moms" and "dads," as victims are known in the confidence trade. These, too, are thriving scams. Ever since some saloon bouncer with thespian talent put on a phony cop's badge and arrested a pederast for purposes of extortion, thieves have made the city's streets their stage.

The police estimate that of all the con games perhaps a third were reported to them. In 1985 about 1,000 people claimed they were victimized — three a day — with a similar number in 1986. During both years, 635 victims reported losing $1.9 million in "handkerchief switches" and 675 reported losing $5.5 million in "pigeon drops." One elaborate pigeon drop — which Kelly claimed was "the largest in the history of this city, probably in the country, and the world" — had netted $2.5 million from 25 victims.

There were so many pockets picked in New York City that officials would not even venture to guess the amount of money stolen. "Pickpockets come out like the crocuses when the weather gets warm," said one Manhattan detective. "They grow wherever there's a crowd." Another detective said that as many as 200 pickpockets fan out each day in the vast network of city buses and subways. "They

own the Madison Avenue bus," he added, referring to a route that runs through Manhattan's fashionable Upper East Side.

Working in teams, a "hook" will extract a wallet from a pocket while a "stall or "blocker" will distract the victim by bumping him. Ideally, the hook will pass the wallet to a "bank" to keep from being caught with evidence. Some teams are quite inventive. A blocker, often a woman, may stop someone to tell him he has a gob of mustard on the back of his coat. When the victim sets down his bag of purchases or attaché case to check, the hook will grab it. Many women have had their handbags stolen in department store toilets because female pickpockets have reached over the stall door and lifted the bag from the door peg. The stores finally decided to remove the pegs. The pickpockets simply bought stick-on pegs and re-installed them.

"The masters of the pickpocket trade in this city are the Colombians because they're relentless," Kelly said. "Once they pick out a victim, they don't quit. They'll stalk that victim until they make the hit. They're extremely aggressive. A lot of pickpockets will lose their nerve. Not the Colombians."

Even so, Kelly scoffed at stories that masterful dips have been trained at "the school of the ten bells" in Bogota, Colombia. "I've heard about that place. That it's run by veteran pickpockets too old to work the street. That it costs $3,000 for two months. That to graduate you have to hit 10 pockets on a dummy without ringing a bell rigged to each pocket. As far as I know, it's a myth. I've never seen any hard evidence that this school exists."

Kelly was readier to believe that three-card monte dealers can steadily make as much as $1,000 a week. A variation of the old pea-under-a-shell game, three-card monte is supposed to have originated two centuries ago in Mexico City. It reached New Orleans by the 1860s and New

York some decades later. It was still the most easily visible scam in Manhattan, particularly during lunchtime hours when office workers crowded the streets.

"We talk to money hustlers who say they've made $800 to $900 in a day, and sometimes more," Kelly said. "And I believe it."

Consider Billie. A slick piece of work beneath a woolen watchman's cap and heavy blue pea coat, she was tossing cards — two black 10s and a red Queen — on top of an empty cardboard carton at the center of a crowd in Times Square. Her rap-style spiel couldn't compete with the megaphone volume of the born-again preacher half a block away, but she had attracted enough pedestrians to surround her four deep.

"Come on, baby, make your play," she rapped. "Red you win, black you lose. You 'n' me ain't got all day."

What the crowd didn't know was that her rap signaled the position of the winning "ticket," as the cards are called. And her shill, a pencil-thin black man with a stylish goatee, was standing at the makeshift tabletop ("the plate") furiously slapping down $20 bills from a fistful of cash. Every time Billie rapped out the word "play," it meant the red Queen would be tossed to the right.

In another rap — "Come on, baby, make your bet. You gonna send me into debt." — the key word "bet" meant the red Queen would be tossed left. In a third rap — "Come on, baby, make your move. You 'n' me are in the groove." — the word "move" indicated the red Queen would be tossed in the middle.

It may not have been poetry, but the shill had won $80 at this point, and he talked up the game. "I'm a betting man," he bantered. "You look like a lady's man," Billie replied.

Two suckers each pulled $100 from their pockets. Billie now resorted to sleight of hand, which is really at the heart of the con. She collected the three cards from the plate and made it obvious that the red Queen was on top.

Then she dealt again, seemingly tossing the top card to the right. Both suckers bet it and both lost.

Billie had actually dealt the "underthrow" (sometimes called the "natural"), which made it appear that the top card had been tossed onto the plate. In fact, the bottom card had slid out. (There is also an "overthrow," in which the top card slides out, and the "hype," which makes the sucker think he has seen the underthrow, but he hasn't.)

If the crowd was not betting, she would "put in the lug" (or "go to the dog ear"). This meant the red Queen would suddenly develop a bent corner, allowing players to believe they could identify it. But the dog-eared card would invariably turn out to be a losing bet because Billie's trained fingers managed to straighten out the Queen during the shuffle and bend the corner of a black 10.

So far, this had been a hot crowd. The action, which was only 20 minutes old, had already netted $140, and one customer was plunging heavily. He was down $60 and trying to recoup with pyramid bets, a sure loser. But a voice at the edge of the crowd yelled, "Slide!" Which was code for "Police!" Billie kicked over the carton, sending the cards flying, and walked off in a hurry. The shill lingered, then drifted off in the opposite direction. The plunger seemed to be weighing his options. But he had none.

Billie ducked into a coffee shop and would regroup later with her shill and the lookout who gave the warning. A proper monte team, she told me, has two lookouts (also called "slides"). But she was short-handed today. The team planned to work Herald Square (the convergence of 34th Street, Sixth Avenue, and Broadway) for the late-afternoon shoppers near Macy's and then move downtown to Wall Street before the evening rush hour to catch homeward-bound stock traders.

At 31, Billie was a seasoned dealer with a dozen years on the street. Born in Louisiana, Billie had skin the color of milk chocolate and shining black eyes. She claimed her family had made a living from con games at least as far back as her grandfather and that she had learned how to deal three-card monte from an uncle. "I came north with my older brother when I was 10," she said, which explained her lack of a deep-South accent. Growing up in Harlem, where they had relatives, Billie and her brother never finished high school. "He's doin' time in Attica," she said.

Billie claimed to have $40,000 saved, and when she has $50,000 she's moving to Los Angeles. "The monte hustle has been good to me, better than turning tricks. I got my own car and my own apartment. And I don't need no pimp."

Although stopped many times, she said she had only been arrested twice in the past year for "facilitating gambling," a misdemeanor that carries a maximum penalty of a year in jail and a $1,000 fine. "I never did time," she said. If a cop on the beat catches a monte game in action, he usually issues a ticket. "It ends up costing fifty, a hundred bucks." Asked whether she had any qualms about cheating suckers, she found the question ridiculous. "Are you kiddin' me? They'd beat me every time they could. And lemme tell you somethin' else, honey, my real name ain't Billie."

As good as Billie was at her game, three-card monte is not even close to the top of the street-scam hierarchy. That distinction belongs to the pigeon drop con or the pocketbook drop — as in, "Gee, madam, did you drop this pocketbook?"

Before madam realizes it, she is being drawn into a confidence game that may fleece her of thousands of dollars. Generally, victims of the pigeon drop are elderly women who are so thoroughly bamboozled that it is not uncommon for them to give up their entire life savings.

The game tends to work like this: A con artist, most often a woman, comes up to the victim after "finding" a a handbag or attaché case. They look inside and find cash, jewels, or securities — always bogus — with a note indicating that the contents are part of some dubious enterprise frequently having to do with news events. The note, known as the "hit slip," can be fairly unsubtle. One note recently confiscated by the bunko squad read: "Dear Ramad, This is the secret money I collected from our friends in the U.S. to help our cause in Lebanon. Be careful and deliver it to our people."

A second con artist joins the victim and the first con. Usually a man, he is full of solicitude. The first con artist will tell the second, "Look what we found." This draws the victim deeper into the scam. There is a vexing issue. What should they do with their find? Surely there must be some obligation to seek the owner. Well, it just so happens that the second con works for an attorney. Why don't they call him on the phone and get some advice? There will be calls back and forth. Invariably, the victim learns that the contents of the bag may be shared with the finder, provided she puts up "good faith" money for a short time in case the owner turns up and must be paid.

"This sounds like a cute game," Lt. Kelly said. "It may not be logical at times, but it doesn't have to be. There are all kinds of complications and misdirections, depending on the particular circumstance. But it is always a heartless game, a cruel game. These cons have missed their calling. They should've been actors. That's how convincing they are. And they've got an answer for every question and every doubt. They're way ahead of the victim. Many of them learn the game in prison. Sometimes they'll have the whole scenario written down for them on an instruction sheet. It will always be a team of man and woman, an approach, an 'attorney' on the phone, and 'good faith' money."

In November 1985, six imaginative swindlers refined the pigeon drop to an art, playing it like an elaborate variation on a theme and carrying it to new heights. Their con game netted them an estimated $2.5 million from 25 New Yorkers in a month, police believed. One victim gave up $100,000 on the street and flew to Palm Beach, Florida, to wire-transfer $150,000 more from securities she cashed in there. One Brooklyn woman gave up $200,000. But the biggest loser was an elderly widow who lived on Park Avenue at one of the poshest addresses in Manhattan. She cashed in a coin collection worth $510,000 and turned it over to the swindlers as good faith money along with $200,000 from liquidated shares of stock. It was the largest pigeon drop on record.

These cons worked their scam with lavish props. The widow was approached near her home by a uniformed chauffeur who got out of a Mercedes limousine. The leather portfolio he "found" contained Iranian securities and cash. After soliciting her help in opening the portfolio, he dialed his "employer" on the limousine phone for advice. His boss not only turned out to be an "attorney," but informed them that in the event the securities proved negotiable she might very well be a legal beneficiary of the find. At the chauffeur's request, she gave his employer her name, address, and phone number, and was told she would be notified of the outcome in a week to 10 days.

The woman said that at that moment she never expected to hear of the matter again. A week and a half later, however, she received a phone call from the attorney telling her that she was very fortunate. The securities had not been claimed, and they were valued at $7 million. The cash in the portfolio came to another $200,000. She was entitled to a share as one of the finders. But there was a problem. The securities could only be cashed in Iran. That meant the Internal Revenue Service would be alerted as soon as they were cashed, and their lucky find would be taxed as straight income.

What they must do instead was show that the money was the result of capital gains from an investment because that would be taxed at a much lower rate. If she had stocks or bonds or jewelry or perhaps a gold collection she could sell, then they could put that money in a safe deposit box and use the receipts to prove that she had converted her assets into cash. Later, when they divided up the money from the Iranian securities, it would be made to appear that her share came from the conversion of assets.

The widow was told, furthermore that she could not breathe a word of her good fortune to anyone because of the risk of tipping off the IRS. The attorney proved to be such a thoughtful benefactor that on discovering she was not in the best of health he assigned his secretary to be her constant nurse and companion. In effect, the victim was being guarded around the clock while receiving continuing phone calls from the attorney to keep her hooked.

Inevitably, there comes a time in all pigeon drops when the victim must put up good faith money. These swindlers rented adjoining suites in the Waldorf-Astoria, ostensibly to count the proceeds from the sale of the Iranian securities. The widow was told to bring the money from her liquidated assets and the key to the safety deposit box that she'd been asked to rent. After the money from the find was counted, they would divide it, put it in money bags, and deposit the bags in the safety box.

Still further, they would leave all the money in the box for a year. This would be sufficient time to prove to the IRS that the widow's share of the $7.2 million had come from long-term capital gains, thus qualifying for the lower tax rate.

To safeguard against any premature withdrawal of the money by either party, the attorney also told the widow that he would keep the key to the deposit box. He couldn't open the box without her signature. She couldn't open the box without the key. It didn't matter anyway, of course, because the money counted in the suite from the Iranian bonds was all counterfeit. The victim's money — more than $700,000 — was switched on her in identical money bags provided by the attorney's confederate in the adjoining suite. In fact, the money-bag switch was simply a variation on what "saw dust men" used to do when they hooked a big buyer of currency. They would get the buyer to a hotel where they had taken adjoining rooms. With the help of a trick desk that had a sliding panel in the back, an accomplice would reach into the desk from the next room and substitute money bags after the real money was counted.

"This widow didn't know she'd been victimized until we sent two detectives over to her apartment," Kelly recounted. "It took them over an hour to convince her she's been caught in a pocketbook drop. On her calendar she had marked the date a year from the day the money went into her safety deposit box."

Four of the swindlers eventually were arrested and convicted of bilking the widow and five other elderly ladies of $1.2 million. Only $74,000 was ever recovered, according to Kelly, who believed two other crooks in the scam were never caught. And what happened to the $1.9 million stolen by the same ring from 19 other victims? Also missing. The four scammers, who were now in prison, agreed to make restitution of $200,000 and received sentences of up to five years on fraud and banking violations.

All con games are related in terms of street psychology. The little sister to the pigeon drop is the handkerchief switch. In this scam, an out-of-towner — a foreign sailor, for instance, or a refugee — will approach a pedestrian to ask for help finding some obscure or nonexistent rooming house. Recently, Betty Horowitz (her name has been changed), a 20-year-old Columbia University student, was approached near the Morningside Heights campus on the Upper West Side of Manhattan by a black man who claimed to be a ship stowaway from South Africa.

"He had an accent and he was very jumpy," she recalled. "I really must have looked naïve. I asked him what's wrong. He told me that he was wary of dogs. He said that in his country the police trained their dogs to attack blacks, which I'm sure is true. His act was so good that when a woman came by walking a miniature poodle he nearly jumped into my arms."

While the stowaway was telling her of his plight, a seccond man came along and struck up a conversation with them. The man, apparently a stranger but in fact a second con, said he knew of the rooming house that the stowaway was seeking. But it was in a pretty seedy neighborhood. He suggested that the stowaway should let Betty hold his money for him or put it in a bank.

"Well, this guy really got paranoid," she said. "He said he didn't trust banks. In his country blacks lost their money if they put it in a bank. I told him it was different here. He didn't believe me. He wanted me to prove it. So I showed him. I walked into my bank and took money out of my account. I actually took out $300. I can't believe it."

Still unconvinced because Betty was white, the stowaway pulled a handkerchief from his pocket and asked her to hold it for him. Then, to prove *he* trusted *her* — a canny reversal — he offered to put his money in with hers. "He told me, 'Let me show you what we do in my country.'" The stowaway wrapped their money together inside the handkerchief, opened his shirt, and put the handkerchief inside. "It was sort of under his arm," Betty remembered. "Then he took it out and gave it back to me. He insisted that I carry it in the same place until he got back. I thought he was just being paranoid again."

Needless to say, Betty never saw the switch that was made inside his shirt, never saw the stowaway again or her $300. When she finally unwrapped the handkerchief, she discovered a "Michigan bankroll," which is a wad of paper covered top and bottom with two real bills. "The guy read her," Kelly said. "He played on her sympathies, everything from how she felt about apartheid to how she felt about this country."

Still, when it comes to exploiting a victim's naiveté, the ultimate con must be the "phony cop comeback." Con artists who have scored a pigeon drop or a handkerchief switch often know their target has more money ripe for plucking. So they will sell Polaroid snapshots of themselves to other cons, who will then knock on the victim's door and play phony cops.

The comeback works this way: We understand you've been the target of a con game. We think we've caught the people. We have them down at the station house. They show the snapshots. Are these the people? Of course they are. We think one of the tellers at the bank where you withdrew your money was working with them. The law says all cash withdrawals of $10,000 (or whatever amount the victim lost) must be reported to the bank manager. We don't think this teller reported it, which makes him a suspect. What we'd like you to do is to go back to the same teller and make another withdrawal. Don't worry. We've already alerted the bank. This time it won't be your money being withdrawn, it will be the bank's. We want to see what the teller does. You must come right out of the bank and give us the money in this bag. It is an evidence bag. It will preserve the teller's fingerprints on the bills in case of a trial.

"You'd be surprised how often we see the phony cop comeback," Kelly said. "These cons use people up and throw them away like an old mop. A lot of you guys in the press glorify con artists. Like that movie with Redford and Newman. What's it called? 'The Sting.' Complete bullshit. The only con men I ever met are a bunch of miserable little pricks."

TRANSATLANTIK, 1987

Underworld

WHEN ALBERTO SICILIA-FALCON was arrested in the bedroom of his Mexico City apartment, he reached for his checkbook on the night table, tore off a check, and wrote in six zeros. Then he handed it to the Mexican police commander and said, "Put any number you like in front of the zeros and get the hell out of here."

Falcon, an international drug trafficker, could well afford the bribe. Among his many bankbooks later found in his Tijuana fortress, two Swiss accounts in one Zurich bank listed assets of $266 million [the equivalent of $1.4 billion today]. His top security man, a professional assassin who had perfected his trade in Vietnam with the infamous Phoenix Program, had claimed before the raid that Falcon's payroll of bribed officials came to $16 million a year.

This time the bribe was declined. Meanwhile, a security card found in Falcon's wallet identified him as a top official of Mexico's domestic and foreign intelligence operations. The card — made of green metal, bordered in gold, and engraved with Falcons photograph — could not have been obtained without influence reaching into the inner sanctum of the Mexican government.

Other evidence subsequently linked him not only to the most ruthless and powerful network of cocaine suppliers in Colombia, Bolivia, and Peru, but with the American Central Intelligence Agency, the Portuguese secret police, Cuban intelligence, weapons deals, guerrilla groups, and top government officials of Guatemala, El Salvador, and Honduras, whom he ferried around on his private Learjet.

Furthermore, narcotics agents working for CENTAC — the Central Tactical Program, a secret unit of the American Drug Enforcement Administration established to investigate and take down drug traffickers — learned from informants that Falcon was conspiring to seize control of the tiny country of Belize (formerly British Honduras, adjacent to Guatemala), with the ultimate goal of gaining control of Mexico itself and possibly all of Central America.

Although the handsome, Cuban-born Falcon was scarcely out of his 20s, and his political ambitions seemed preposterously egomaniacal, they were not to be taken lightly. Falcon already had the entire city bureaucracy of Guadalajara on his payroll. And he had a grip on the whole province of San Luis Potosi through his close ally and reputed lover, Gaston Santos, a wealthy, politically connected bullfighter-movie star, whose father was revered as a military hero of the Mexican Revolution. Santos's family position and his private army of 1,500 men had turned the province, just northeast of Mexico City, into a personal fiefdom.

Indeed, in the wake of Falcon's arrest, the PRI (the Institutional Revolutionary Party, which has controlled the Mexican presidency since 1929) had to withdraw its plan to nominate Mario Moya Palencia, the chief of Gobernacion, as its candidate to succeed President Luis Echeverria because his association with Falcon was revealed. (The PRI nominated Jose Lopez Portillo instead, and he was elected.)

"Had Falcon not been arrested, Palencia would almost certainly have become president," says James Mills, who began investigating what he calls 'the underground empire' in 1980 and who recently published these mind-boggling revelations in a massive exposé entitled *The Underground Empire*. As he sips a scotch-and-water at Costello's, a noted Manhattan saloon favored by local reporters, Mills asks knowingly, "Where would that have put Falcon?"

A former United Press reporter who made his reputation in the 1960s as a *Life* magazine writer covering drugs and cops, Mills looks at first like a tall, earnest, Ivy League professor with neatly trimmed hair and horn-rimmed glasses. But when he drops his glasses on the table and takes off his jacket and tie, muttering that he never wears "this damned uniform" except on visits to New York City, he might well pass for a tough, sophisticated narcotics cop himself.

Mills likes to point out that everyone has heard of Mafia bosses such as Joseph Bonanno and Sam Giancana, but that few people have heard of Falcon, whose hunger for power he compares with Hitler's. Even today, a decade after his arrest, Falcon continues to wield influence from his Mexico City prison cell, where he receives visitors and lives as though under mere house detention.

"One thing I learned about people like Falcon is that they're demonic," says Mills, who gained the confidence of Dennis Dayle, chief of CENTAC (said to be the most unorthodox, effective, and least-known international police organization in the world) and was allowed to travel with Dayle's agents in Latin America, Asia, Europe, and the U.S.,

Mills often managed on his own to get close to CENTAC targets as well as confidential informants.

"I really think there is evil in these underworld people, and in this whole underground world," he adds. "And I got to the point where I believed it was a separate realm of demons."

It concerns the 54-year-old author of seven previous books, including *Panic in Needle Park* and *Report to the Commisioner,* that believing in demons may make him sound "like a science-fiction kook," and that the astonishing information he recounts in *The Underground Empire: Where Crime and Governments Embrace* may seem like the stuff of adventure cartoons.

Will people snicker in disbelief, he wonders, when they hear about "the Buck Rogers-ish laser-sighted super-rifle" that Falcon hoped to make use of in his quest for power?

The rifle, called the MC101, fires faster than the M16 and carries twice as many clips. An attached rocket, which has no recoil because of its unique design, can knock out a tank in one shot. It also can fire a round ball carrying an explosive charge equal to a 105 mm howitzer, putting the firepower of an artillery piece in the hands of an infantryman. A company of soldiers armed with that super-rifle could lay down a barrage equal to a battalion of howitzers.

"Any man with this weapon is equal to 50 men with a conventional weapon," its designer, James Morgan, told Falcon. All he needed to finance manufacturing it was a $10-million investment.

It doesn't take much arithmetic to realize that an army of 1,500 men equipped with this weapon would give him the equivalent of 75,000 troops. Nor does it take much to figure out that a group of 100 guerrillas, say in El Salvador, would be the equivalent of a 5,000-man fighting force.

The fact that Falcon was particularly cruel buttressed Mills's belief in demons. Furthermore, the fact that Falcon was also a homosexual who took an 11-year-old boy for his catamite did little to diminish it. And not least, the fact that Falcon was part of a mysterious devil-worship cult set Mills to thinking even darker thoughts.

"I wanted to know a lot more about the devil worship," Mills says. But there just wasn't any way to find out. The guy who brought him into the cult was dead, and Falcon was not about to discuss it."

The ultimate confirmation of a perverse demonology at work was perhaps Mills's discovery that Falcon had penned a tract portraying himself as a victim of persecution who, in his delusional words, "continues to feel nostalgia for a just and humane society." Certainly Dayle and his Centac agents were convinced that Falcon's relentless lust for power came much closer to realization than seems credible or comfortable, although key Centac agents who worked the case were thinking less of Satan than hints that the CIA was protecting Falcon.

"Every time we turned around, somebody was rear-ending us," one of those agents, Rick Gorman, told Mills. "Some invisible force seemed to be doing everything to screw us up." When Mills asked Dayle if Falcon was ever affiliated with the CIA, Dayle replied, "There's no question in my mind." And when Mills asked Dayle if he believed a report that Falcon had offered CIA assassination jobs to his hitman, Dayle credited it "absolutely."

Some CENTAC agents suspected the CIA itself finally decided that Falcon was getting too big and may have surfaced informants whom CENTAC found and exploited to bring him down. Dayle did not exactly discourage this notion. He admitted to Mills that he himself had done work for the CIA in Beirut, where he had spent several years during the 1960s as the Federal Bureau of Narcotics agent-in-charge. Attached to the American embassy there, he often met directly with the security chiefs of Lebanon, Turkey, and Syria. He also traveled widely in the Middle East, disguised as a high-level narcotics trafficker.

"My whole life experience tells me that the ultimate motivation for the world drug traffic by its top purveyors is not profiteering," Dayle told me. "That is a very high objective, but the ultimate goal is power. And Falcon is the classic case of power for power's sake. He very definitely wanted his own country. That is absolutely real. What is just as real," adds Doyle, who is 57 and now retired from CENTAC, "is that he almost did get his own country but for the fact that we were able to counter-manipulate the kind of power that got him as far as he did. And we were able to dismantle him by embarrassing the Mexican authorities into placing him in custody. I give you this: Sicilia-Falcon would have set himself up either as the actual leader or as the power behind the throne of a Central American sovereignty, and in all likelihood his representatives would have been accepted diplomatically. We would have exchanged ambassadors with a complete thug."

In that context, Falcon simply would have risen to the level of Panama army commander Gen. Manuel Noriega, who probably ranks as the single-largest cocaine trafficker — and certainly the most prominent — among Central American officials. Even the last Panama dictator Gen. Omar Torrijos, a formidable trafficker in his own day, may not compare with him. Some people suspect an active CIA involvement with Noreiga's drug deals, Mills says. But he believes it is more of a blind-eye arrangement as a tradeoff for intelligence benefits.

"Say I'm the CIA station chief in Panama," he theorizes. "I meet you. Your name is Gen. Noriega. Wonderful. You run the country. You're giving intelligence about Cuba and Nicaragua. Fantastic. You're allowing me to put in agents of influence. Colossal. Nothing could be better. Am I going to deny myself all that you provide me with because I don't like you being in the dope business? Or am I going to forget I ever knew you were in it and keep my channel open?"

Columbia, which processes 80 percent of the world's cocaine, and Bolivia and Peru, which account for 95 percent of the coca plants, certainly manage to maintain diplomatic relations with the United States. Yet the cocaine industry accounts for more of their revenue than any other export and could not operate without the active participation of highly placed officials. It's equally true — and not new — that corrupt Thai and Burmese officials participate in the heroin traffic of Asia's so-called Golden Triangle without damaging their diplomatic relations with the U.S. The private Yunnanese armies, which are the backbone of the opium supply routes in the Triangle, operate not only with official complicity, but also under the sponsorship of the CIA and competing intelligence agencies.

Now consider Pakistan President Gen. Mohamed Zia al-Haq, a different sort of case but with similar implications. According to Dayle, Zia obviously meets the requirements of American foreign policy in his sphere of influence by keeping the perceived enemies of the West at bay. "To do this, Zia needs moneys," Dayle says, "and one of the easiest ways for a Pakistani strongman to get money is to siphon huge sums from the traditional drug traffic."

If there are limits to the amount of American foreign aid that can be spared for Zia, it is the CIA's role to unofficially get him money, Dayle says, speaking "theoretically." Thus, the CIA facilitates drug traffic to funnel the profits to him.

"What you save in the foreign aid budget that would have gone to Zia can now be spent to spread your influence elsewhere," Dayle says. "It is very pragmatic." While he admits, "I can't put evidence on a consul's table," Dayle emphasizes. "My own conclusion — professionally — is that Zia is or has been a direct recipient of drug megadollars in his rise to power."

Dayle also points out that the CIA is surely not responsible for the worldwide drug traffic. Furthermore, drug revenues are pocketed by officials of all political persuasions, including enemies of the West. He has no doubt that Cuba's President Fidel Castro is a trafficker "to a more provable degree" than Libya's Col. Muammar el-Qaddafi.

And Qaddafi "is absolutely a beneficiary" of the drug trade.

As for Palestine Liberation Organization Chairman Yasir Arafat, Dayle says, "He certainly enjoys profits from the drug trade. In my own view that makes him a drug dealer." It is worth noting that during the 1970s CENTAC mounted an attack on Middle Eastern heroin traffickers and listed Arafat as one of its major targets. A confidential informant pinpointed Arafat as the original owner of a load of Turkish heroin for sale to the Mafia in New York, Mills says. But CENTAC could not verify the report.

Dayle and his agents eventually found it just as fruitless trying to prosecute Lu Hsu-shui, an elderly Chinese gangster who lives quietly in Bangkok and, according to Mills, "runs what is probably the largest narcotics organization on earth." For that matter, CENTAC could never shut down the Thai narcotics king Poonsiri Chanyasak, who operates with the quasi-official support of the Laos government and is known in Asian politic circles as Laos's "minister of heroin."

Given the astronomical sums generated by the worldwide traffic in cocaine, heroin, and marijuana, it is easy to understand why governments, corrupt officials, intelligence Agencies, guerrilla movements, terrorists, and ambitious criminals such as Falcon exploit it as a virtually infinite resource.

According to classified CIA and National Security Agency documents unearthed by Mills, the worldwide drug traffic reaps annual revenues of more than half a trillion dollars. That is three times the value of all the U.S. currency in circulation. People spend more on illegal drugs than on food or housing or clothing or any other product or service. The drug trade is worth more than the total goods and services of all but the six largest industrialized nations.

"Drug profits secretly stockpiled in countries competing for the business draw interest exceeding three million dollars per hour," Mills says, and he is considering doing a book on drug revenues alone. "Nobody puts dirty money in Switzerland anymore," he adds. "It's a sieve. They put it in Panama, Hong Kong, and Lichtenstein."

Falcon was so rich he used to lay out half a million dollars' worth of cocaine for guests at his lavish orgies. One of his secrete warehouses — and he had several — held 100 tons of marijuana worth $34 million wholesale. Some 19 tractor-trailers were counted picking up 57 tons for delivery in just one month. And marijuana was only part of his smuggling operation, which concentrated on the much more profitable cocaine trade. One informant told Mills how he and others were tasked with counting and stacking one week's worth of cash. The count came to slightly more than $7.4 million and took them ten hours to do it.

"It's almost impossible to put a dollar figure on how much Falcon had," Rich Gorman, now a DEA supervisor says. "His wealth seems to have no end to it. I happen to know he had some bank accounts in names other than his real one. It reflected a considerable amount of money in Mexican banks as well as foreign ones. But I was never advised how much or which bank accounts were seized by the Mexican authorities."

Although Falcon was more interested in power than wealth, as Dayle, Mills, and Gorman agree, Falcon's two Swiss accounts of $266 million by themselves would have placed him among the Fortune 500's wealthiest individuals.

Another world-class drug dealer taken down by CENTAC who could have made the list was Donald Steinberg. Hardly a famous name in the annals of crime, Steinberg had no political ambitions, just the boyhood dream of running a marijuana company doing a billion dollars a year, Mills says.

This Chicago-born smuggler almost reached that goal while still in his 30s. Importing $20-million freight loads at a time, he had so much cash on hand that he began stuffing it, uncounted, in samsonite suitcases. Whenever he needed to know how much money he had, he simply counted suitcases and estimated them at $500,000 each. Money wasn't even called money. It was called "go," as in: "Give him some go." At one point on his city-to-city collection runs, Steinberg was flying around the U.S. in his Learjet with $47 million in suitcases and footlockers.

Before Steinberg was finally captured, police got an idea of his wealth from a raid at a Fort Lauderdale, Fla., motel, where he and his associates were staying. They found $1.4 million in several suitcases and a pad with Steinberg's notations indicating that he'd netted $35 million for a three-month smuggling-and-distribution operation in a single city. "He was," says Mills, "the Henry Ford of the international marijuana industry."

Unlike Falcon, Steinberg avoided cocaine smuggling because, among other reasons, he feared violence. Dealing with Colombian cocaine traffickers was virtually a guarantee of violence. He didn't much like guns either, and cocaine and guns go together. His lack of political ambition also tended to keep him out of arms deals such as the $250-million weapons cache that Falcon, Santos, and others are supposed to have assembled with CIA backing for an anti-Communist coup d'état in Portugal that never materialized.

"The weapons in this deal made Morgan's super-rifle look like something found in a Cracker Jack box," Mills says. "Falcon, the Portuguese, and the CIA were discussing light machine guns, artillery pieces, amphibious vehicles, jeeps, and 100,000 rounds of ammunition — all to be delivered and paid FOB (freight on board) the Azores."

The deal, which was to earn Falcon and his associates a $25-million commission, remains shrouded in mystery. But some fragmentary information is known, Mills says, and in any case helps shed light on Falcon's utility as a CIA weapons conduit.

Falcon was said to be a personal friend of Gen. Spinola, head of the military junta that overthrew the Portuguese dictatorship in 1974 and later resigned under pressure from leftist officers. Falcon told an associate that the chief of Portugal's secret service, as well as Gaston Santos — who fought bulls from horseback, Portuguese-style, and had his own nefarious connections — had asked him to supply the heavy weapons for the coup. Falcon obtained a CIA weapons brochure and took it to Spain, where he showed it to a Portuguese intelligence officer and to the Portuguese president in exile in Madrid.

One of the peculiar characteristics of the underground empire is that just when you reach what you think is the highest rung of power, you discover whole new vistas above it. So how high up was Falcon?

"Well, there are really two scales of measurement in terms of his strata," Dayle says. "One places him only halfway up the ladder because he had sources of supply and criminal confederates who were more highly placed within the drug trade. The other scale measures what he had in terms of political power and actual physical resources. And there he was at the top or near the top. He was much higher on that scale than the people who exceeded him within the drug trade. On the scale of buying and selling drugs, I think he was where he wanted to be. He could have been a larger supplier had he wanted."

Who then are the biggest traffickers?

Mills leans back in the booth at Costello's and smiles. Let's see, he says. There's Gilberto Rodriguez, "one of the heavy hitters, who is about to be bonded out of jail in Colombia." There's Jorge Ochoa, "who is walking around in Colombia right now." And there's Santiago Ocampo, "also walking around." Courtesy of the Colombian government, he might have added.

"Colombia prevented Rodriguez and Ochoa from being extradited to the U.S. when they got locked up in Spain not long ago," Mills notes. "I wonder what that cost in bribes."

Then there's always Eduard Tascon-Moran, "one of the grand old men," who used to be Panama Gen. Torrijos's cocaine connection. Tascon used to trade cocaine for guns in Miami, Mills says. He routed the guns through Torrijos and supplied them to guerrilla groups in South America. Like Falcon, he connected with politicians, penetrated intelligence agencies, and hobnobbed with diplomats on several continents. But he also was much closer to the source of cocaine. "Whether Tascon is still alive, I'm not sure," Mills says.

It's interesting that when a Colombian newspaper ran excerpts from *The Underground Empire* over two days a few months ago, Cali (Colombia's third-largest city) suddenly found itself without that newspaper. Apparently jeeploads of armed men drove around the city buying up the paper at the distribution points, Mills says. Maybe it's only a coincidence that Tascon reportedly had almost every public official in Cali on his payroll. Or perhaps Ochoa and Ocampo didn't like seeing their photographs published with the excerpts.

Finally we come to Mr. Big himself, although not much has been heard from him lately. His name is Alfonso Rivera. Born 55 years ago in Honduras, he is now a Peruvian citizen. According to Mills, a CENTAC analyst said Rivera supplied "all key traffickers, in Colombia, all of them in Mexico, most of them in the United States, and a lot of them in Europe." He became "the largest single cocaine source in the world," Mills says.

One Rivera lab discovered in a resort near Lima, Peru, had processed seven tons of coca paste into more than two tons of cocaine crystal during two years of operation. That came to $100 million wholesale, or about a billion dollars retail. And Rivera had many labs. He wasn't joking when he named his enterprise the International Narcotics Organization. INO smuggled coca paste and coca base among Peru, Ecuador, and Columbia on Peruvian tour buses, which always had a uniformed army officer aboard to smooth the border crossings.

Once the paste reached Cali, or Guayaquil in Ecuador, where Rivera had once managed a Coca-Cola bottling company, it was converted to crystal and shipped to Mexico and the United States. Rivera was also shipping from three Colombian ports. "Customs officials were so much a part of Rivera's organization," Mills points out, "that they worked from two tariffs — one for legitimate cargo, another for cocaine."

But even Rivera needed a supplier of coca plants. His was the Parades family in the Peruvian coca-trading town of Tingo Maria, at the edge of the Amazon. The sprawling Parades family, with rival branches, owns vast coca plantations, and you can't get any closer to the source than that.

"The only trafficking organizations higher than the Parades and their counterparts in other countries are the national governments themselves," Mills says. "Some of the groups change. One lays low for a while. Another takes its place. But the result is the same."

Mills estimates that there are perhaps no more than 50 traffickers at the very pinnacle of underground power worldwide. Yet their influence is so entrenched that whole nations are undermined. "When I hear Ed Meese, the attorney general of the United States, saying that drug trafficking is no longer a problem in the Mexican government," Mills declares, "I don't know whether I'm dreaming or Ed Meese is dreaming."

As if to underscore his point, The New York Times reported on Oct. 10, 1986, that Mexico's chief of the security police, along with the head of Mexico's Interpol office; three provincial governors; a cousin of President Miguel de la Madrid; a federal prosecutor who also happens to be the son of the Defense Minister; and the Defense Minister himself, had all recently been implicated in widespread drug trafficking.

Coming as it does years after the events chronicled in *The Underground Empire*, the latest news sounds like a repeat performance. And so we end what appears to be a never-ending story on a cautionary note: To Be Continued.

TRANSATLANTIK, 1986

EXIT FROM FLEET STREET

NOT FAR FROM HYDE PARK in the sleek intimacy of the Montcalm Hotel foyer, Frederick Forsyth sank into a soft leather couch and ordered a glass of white wine. The barman knew him. So did the concierge and the bellmen. Forsyth had kept appointments there for years, coming up weekly to London from his country home in Surrey, where he had lived since 1979 with his Irish wife, Carrie, a former actress, and their two sons.

"We got a little homesick for the old place," he said. They had returned to England after six years abroad. "We had to put the kids in school someplace. And my parents, who are getting older and frailer, couldn't travel across to Ireland anymore. I'm their only son and the kids are their only grandchildren."

The cozy image of Forsyth as a family man was strange. Lacking the telltale paunch of the married man, and with a drink in hand, Forsyth hardly seemed domesticated in appearance. He looked, at 43, like a military officer in tweeds — lean, fit, almost movie-star handsome, with a tan offset by curly, blondish hair, and a brisk manner suggesting efficiency and authority.

Before becoming the well-known author of best-selling thrillers — *The Day of the Jackal* (1971); *The Odessa File* (1972); *The Dogs of War* (1974); *The Devil's Alternative* (1979) — all of which had earned him millions — he'd once been the youngest fighter pilot in the Royal Air Force. After that he had trotted the globe as a Reuters man, BBC correspondent, and freelance war reporter who tagged along with the mercenary "hard squads" of Africa.

Forsyth looked different, too, from the various dissemblers, shady and otherwise, in *No Comebacks,* the story collection he had just published.

I asked why he had turned to short fiction for the first time in his writing career, especially when story collections were noted for their dismal commercial success. He replied simply: "By default." His agent and his publisher had both asked whether he had a novel for them. He didn't. But he mentioned that he had 10 stories — two written, eight in note form. "The publisher jumped round and said, 'That's enough for a book!'"

In fact, Forsyth did have a novel percolating in his head. but he hadn't set anything down. "If I'm not satisfied, I don't start writing," he said. "I felt that after the large canvas of *The Devil's Alternative* I didn't want to turn in a rather poor potboiler about some kind of payroll heist just to keep the name out front. It would disappoint a hell of a lot of people."

The two stories that Forsyth had finished — "No Comebacks" and "Money With Menaces" — set the tone for the collection. The first was about a bored tycoon who gets more than he bargains for from a hired killer; the second was about a harmless insurance clerk who gives his blackmailers more than they expect. All of the stories, told in quick strokes, turned out to be dominated by themes of revenge, violence, weird coincidence, confidence men and, most of all, by black humor full of ironies.

When I asked Forsyth about his background, he told me he had grown up in Ashford, a small village southeast of London, and was the son of shopkeepers. His father was a furrier, his mother a dressmaker. He recalled living "in a nice middle-class house on a tree-lined avenue" and getting a scholarship to Tonbridge, a boarding school that expected its top graduates to go on to Oxford or Cambridge. Forsyth, who had passed his exams more than a year early, at 17, wanted no part of university.

"I wanted, first, to fly airplanes and, second, to be a reporter," he recalled in his clipped British accent. "I read the usual boy's stuff, but then I moved on mostly to technical manuals. I actually memorized every bird in The Observer's *Book of Birds*. One hundred fifty pages. Then I got *All the World's Aircraft*, which is a thing of about 1,500 pages. In my mid-teens I reached a point where I could probably recognize every plane in the world by its silhouette."

Flying and journalism were absolutely not what the school had in mind for him. "They thought it was beneath the dignity of one of their public school scholars. One ought to have gone into the more respectable professions: stocks and bonds, law, medicine, insurance. I pointed out that it was my life anyway, and I was damned well going to do it. So I did."

Forsyth had one other obsession in his teens — bullfighting — inspired by a reading of Hemingway's *Death in the Afternoon*. With six months to kill until he was old enough for pilot training, Forsyth went to Malaga, Spain, where he spent the time learning cape work from "an old, gimpy ex-bullfighter who had taken one corrida too many."

cigarette, he recounted the events of his life with names, dates, and places as though they had happened yesterday. By 1956 he was flying the Vampire, a RAF jet fighter. Two years later, still not 20, he took his first job as a reporter on a provincial newspaper. Three years later he went to Reuters and was posted to Paris.

"I had been a language student at school," he said. "I spoke French, German, Spanish, and some Russian. Reuters was interested in that. They took me on. Paris was a good break. A guy was called out of the bureau there with bleeding ulcers. So a fellow put his head 'round the door in London and said, 'Anyone here speak French?' I said, 'Moi.' He said, 'All right, you're on your way.'"

Forsyth arrived in Paris in May 1962. Algerian independence was due on July 1. He thus had a ringside seat as the OAS (the Secret Army Organization) terrorized France in protest. His first thriller, *The Day of the Jackal*, which was written eight years later, took that as its subject and wove into it a plot to assassinate Charles de Gaulle, the French president.

The Odessa File, his second thriller, had much the same theme: manhunt. A stationary target is hunted by a mobile hunter who himself is hunted by the target. The suspense is created by who will get to whom first. What astonished readers of *Jackal* was how accurate and credible it seemed.

"Most of my note-taking was mental," Forsythe told me. "People thought I researched for years. What I had in front of me were a half dozen brown envelopes with some notes scribbled on them in the streets of Paris. When I actually sat down to write, I didn't intend to become a novelist. I just happened to be out of work and was financially a little embarrassed.

"I was a freelance just back from Biafra. I had nothing much to do. It was January 1970. It was freezing cold. There was snow on the streets. I didn't have an apartment. I was going down on the sofa in a friend's London flat. It was more than embarrassing. I was really pretty desperate. So I said, 'Hell, I have this idea. I've had it since Paris. I've thought it over in my head but never got around to writing it. I will write it now.' It was all from memory."

How Forsyth became a freelance is instructive. Hired away from Reuters by the BBC, he was assigned to cover Biafra for 10 weeks in July 1967, but he had been hauled back, he said, because his stories predicted a bloody race war and, ultimately, genocide.

"They said, 'Your reports have upset a lot of people and, uh, they're not what they wanted to hear.' I said, 'I'm prepared to back my judgment.' Six months went by and what I had forecast would happen duly began to happen. I said, 'Can I go back?' And they said, 'Absolutely not. We're not covering the story at all.' I said, 'I don't like managed news. I suspect this is managed news. I will not be part of it. I'm off.'"

Word went around Fleet Street one day in 1968 that BBC correspondent Freddie Forsyth had "gone missing." Fellow reporters chortled that Freddie didn't even give three months' notice. "The so-called mystery as to what happened to me was no mystery at all," Forsyth said.

"The BBC was so embarrassed by the whole thing that they declined to release my letter of resignation. I hadn't gone missing at all. I told them where I was going and what I was doing, and why I was doing it.

"I went straight from the BBC house to my apartment, grabbed a suitcase, and took the next flight to Lisbon, and then I went and saw an American arms runner who was flying old Super Connies from Lisbon to Biafra. He sandwiched me between a couple of crates of mortars and we went in that same night."

Forsyth's sudden departure became a two-year odyssey, resulting in his first, little-known book of nonfiction, *The Biafra Story*. It appeared in 1969. It also brought him into close contact with the world of mercenaries in Africa and elsewhere, which would become a matrix for much of his later fiction, notably *The Dogs of War*.

"I was trying to make a living down there, and the mercenaries were where the action was," he recounted. "I went and saw the Biafran general [Odumengwu] Ojukwu. I said, 'Do you mind if I tag along?' He said, 'What do you want to go with them for?' I said, 'To file stories about what's going on. You know the newspapers aren't going to buy your propaganda bulletins.' They were by and large as fanciful as the Nigerian propaganda bulletins, and they were written by clerks in offices miles from the front.

"The only copy real newspapers would buy from a freelance was on-site eyewitness action combat stories. At that time the story of the children dying of starvation had not yet begun to happen. That really began around June 1968, when the 12-month lack of protein began to hit in a big way, and you saw skeletons walking around called kids."

As might be expected, Forsyth is very much "a man's writer." Romance hardly made an appearance in his work. When it did, it was rarely descriptive or even credible. He believed it was not necessary — not "for my kind of stuff," he said — and he refused "to put in a couple of gratuitous pages of screwing."

"I don't think it sells one extra copy," Forsyth said. "For Harold Robbins maybe. A book of his with no sex just isn't a Harold Robbins book. It's what his readers expect. I write about romance extremely badly anyway. My wife is the first to say, 'Your sex scenes are pathetic beyond belief.' She doesn't mind the practice, but she feels my descriptions are appalling from a woman's point of view. I concede that. I am not a romantic writer."

Nor was he writing for the ages. Forsyth said there are basically three kinds of writer. The first has a message for humanity. "He will put it over whether the reader likes it or not. I evidently do not have a message." The second is "the compulsive writer." He is unhappy when not flogging away at his typewriting eight hours a day 352 days a year. He will turn out "literally hundreds of books."

"The third guy," Forsyth said, "actually doesn't like being locked away in a small room facing shuttered windows with the sun shining. He is wondering, 'What am I doing in here anyway?' He's really writing to get to the last line of the last chapter. And when it's over he is so bloody relieved! That's me."

Chicago Sun-Times, 1982

THE PROFESSIONAL

THE CRITICS WERE progressively less kind to James Michener. It was a burden he willingly bore. But it was no fun. "Damn it," he told me, "when you've done 10 or 12 books in a row and they've all been enormous best sellers, you at least know *something.*"

It was eight, but why quibble? After 27 books, he was entitled to lose count.

When I spoke to him, he was 73 and as ruddy as a sailor. His high-domed forehead was freckled from the sun. His white fringe of hair was clipped. His manner was brisk but unhurried. His gray-flecked eyes, framed by glasses, were as clear as the day. But his modesty became him most.

Michener's first book, in 1948, a slim collection of stories entitled *Tales of the South Pacific,* didn't appear until he was 40. But despite such a remarkably late start for so prolific an author, he had established himself as one of the most popular storytellers of his time. "I've had good luck," he allowed.

Michener was sitting in a straight-backed chair in a Plaza Hotel suite. His wife of 25 years, Mari Yoriko Sabusawa, was out seeing the town.

"Writing talent is fairly common," he said. "A lot of people have it, and dicey things intervene to determine what level they're going to come in at. I'm a very good professional. But all that means is that I'm eligible. If good luck comes along, I know what to do with it."

Somebody once calculated that Michener's writings — including the films, theatrical productions, and television shows based upon them — had earned the federal government about $35 million in taxes. His latest epic, *The Covenant*, was just out and immediately topped the best seller lists. Good luck seemed to flow from his pen.

"If I relied upon sex, or kinky aberrations, or violence, or sadism, or cheapness, I would be apologetic for the success my books have had," Michener said. Then, with a sort of pride, he noted, "Of the many books I've written, a good third were never best sellers."

Curiously, *Tales of the South Pacific* was not a best seller, despite winning the Pulitzer Prize and serving as the basis for Rodgers and Hammerstein's "South Pacific," one of the most successful Broadway musicals ever. Others that didn't sell were the books on Oriental art (*The Floating World*), politics (*Kent State: What Happened and Why* and *Presidential Lottery*), athletics (*Sports in America*), or sociology (*The Quality of Life*).

The best sellers were the novels, all set in exotic places: *The Bridges at Toko-Ri* (Korea, 1953); *Sayonara* (Japan, 1954); *Hawaii* (1959); *Caravans* (Afghanistan, 1963); *The Source* (the Middle East, 1965); *Iberia* (Spain, 1968); and *Centennial* (the American West, 1974). "I haven't been a Johnny-One-Note," Michener said. "I haven't tried to play the norm. I've had a very wide scatter."

Critics claimed his popularity rested upon his ability to spoon-feed readers a multitude of lessons about the world in a serviceable and pleasurable way. From the very beginning several didactic themes dominated all his fiction: relations between the races; the retribution of war and human cruelty; the birth of nations; the saving grace of work; the obligation of love; the grandeur of nature.

Michener went along with that, but added: "If you get Dickens and Thackeray constantly, as I did in childhood, you must develop a certain sense of narrative — which I think I have to a remarkable degree. That is about the only artistic talent that is unique in my case. I do know how a story ought to be told, and I have a gut feeling when it's going the wrong way. Character, dialogue — all that I leave to others. The average person has no conception of how carefully worked out my books are, how architecturally sound they tend to be. There are a lot of things I can't do. *That*, I think, I can do."

If Michener's fiction has been voluminous in its bulk and epic in its scope, it is because he intuitively shied away from the small books of very concise statement. The hard-boiled prose of *Toko-Ri* and *Sayonara*, which possess the glint of good detective-style fiction though not the subject matter, tempted Michener to go small. But he discarded the idea.

"I wrote *Toko-Ri* to prove I could do it," he recalled. "I probably could write a book like that every year of my life. I hope that doesn't sound arrogant, but I think I could. And I might have a better reputation in the long run if I had. But it just showed me nothing, although I have a great respect for Dashiell Hammett and Raymond Chandler and their type of books. I think I could have moved into their field."

Michener always brimmed with that sort of confidence. He was a born optimist. He would have to have been to survive his poorhouse childhood. Life for Michener began as a foundling on a street in Doylestown, Pennsylvania. He once said he didn't think he would cross the pavement to meet his biological parents, but he insisted to me that his remark did not reflect any bitterness.

"No," he told me, "bitterness I don't have. If you survive these things, you don't brood about them. Now you have to remember that everything I say is postulated on the fact that I did come through it. So maybe it's easy for me to say no bitterness."

Taken off the street by a Quaker widow, Mrs. Mabel Michener, he spent his early years shuttling between her home in Doylestown and Philadelphia, where he delivered the shirts she mended for a living. When money ran out, "this wonderful woman," as Michener described her, was forced to put her family in the county poorhouse until the worst had passed.

By the age of 13 Michener had traveled considerably; by 15 he had hitchhiked west to the Mississippi, north to Maine, south to Florida. He never hesitated to leave home. "I wouldn't think I had the traditional wanderlust," he said. "It was something different. I'm not quite sure what it was. With 35 cents in my pocket, I went to Detroit," he recalled. "In those days — this must have been 1921, 1922 — you would go out on the road and people with cars for the first time would want to show them off. It was very leisurely. They'd pick you up and feed you and put you up in their homes at night. Hell, for $1.35 I would go to the big river. Bakers would give you state bread and you didn't meet brutal types unless you sought them out. I was never courageous in that respect."

His courage was tested in quite another way, though, when his foster mother revealed for the first time that Michener was an orphan. He was in his mid-teens by then and he had had inklings. After all, Mrs. Michener took in many transient waifs. "I'm like everybody else," he said. "I was shattered, torn loose. But it was only for about a week and a half. After 10 days a reasonably healthy person says, 'Now wait a minute. That's a disaster in my life, only I ain't goin' down that road.' Sure there were many points at which I could have gone pretty sour."

Instead, Michener excelled. He became a varsity basketball star and valedictorian of his class. He went on to Swarthmore College on the first scholarship it ever gave, rarely got less than high A in his studies, and graduated *summa cum laude.*

Perhaps it's not surprising that he believes the mystery of his origins is of little consequence. "People have wasted years of their lives trying to figure out where they came from. I think this is an indulgence. But I don't want to belabor people who are engaged in a futile search as if it's going to spring them loose."

Michener paused and gazed out the window at the treetops of Central Park. We'd been talking steadily for nearly an hour. "I see that kind of thing a great deal," he went on. "There are writers who feel that if only they could write a book, somehow their lives would be changed. Hell, you know what happens to the average book? It sells 2,800 copies and it earns $300 a year for the author, and nobody ever hears about it.

"And there you are — you're the same jerk you were before it was published. Well, that's also true if your book sells 100,000 copies. It hasn't modified the life at all and usually doesn't even modify the employment. You still have the same problem of who you are and what you stand for and what you're going to do next."

Michener had spent his life until he was 40 in the backwater of academic publishing as an editor and as a writer for university journals specializing in education. But once he found his métier as a novelist, he never let himself be distracted. He wrote seven days a week, beginning at 7:30 a.m. and ending at about noon. The routine rarely varied either at home in Bucks County, Pennsylvania or at his bungalow in St. Michaels on the Maryland shore. Still, he said, he had lived a vigorous life.

"I've seen people killed off my shoe tops. I've survived three major airplane crashes. I've been in war situations that most people never think of. I've had a major heart attack. None of my friends think of me as macho, but I've seen more violence than any of them."

He said, "the momentous decision to begin a book," though it may have been in preparation for years, always came suddenly and felt like "the closing of a door" behind him. Once he made the decision, all the other books he had may have had in mind would go dead, "never to be revived in the same form."

He said that at his age he often pondered the question of how many years of writing he had left. It was an admission he made stoutly. Without a trace of an old man's vanity, he added: "I don't see a diminution in my intellectual interest or acuity, and I watch that very carefully. As long as that stays with me, I'll continue writing. I've got ideas for the rest of the century, and I'm not kidding about that. I would never lose the drive. I might lose the capacity."

Were that to happen, it seemed to me no writer would have laid down his pen more neatly.

Chicago Sun-Times, 1980

He never did, though. Over the next 17 years until he died, Michener produced a dozen more fiction epics — critics be damned — and another 14 volumes of nonfiction.

HIS SOUTH AFRICA

HE PICKED UP THE PHONE in the limousine whisking him between planes from O'Hare Airport to Chicago's Loop. "It's the first time I have ever had a telephone conversation from a car," he said. It was a first for both of us. There were no cellphones in 1983.

The occasion for our chat was a production of "Master Harold ... and the boys." The play, regarded as a masterpiece, had propelled Athol Fugard into the first rank of living dramatists. Such esteem had bred too many appointments in too little time. Phoning him from my desk in the newsroom seemed the surest way of catching him alone.

Fugard was about to turn 51 later that week. A small, wiry man with a short beard, he was often pictured smoking a pipe. His reputation for modesty preceded him, so

I half expected him to downplay the critical acclaim. Which he did. "I knew enough about my craft as a playwright," he told me, "to know that I had made a good little play. I deliberately use that term, 'good little play,' because it is the only way I will ever refer to it."

Calling it "my youngest born," Fugard said it was "obviously a favorite because it's still suckling at the breast. Otherwise I wouldn't be in America at this moment. But it does come as a surprise to watch an audience, as I have in Minneapolis, stand up at the end of a performance. It makes me a little bit scared."

I thought he would have gotten used to ovations. "Master Harold" had had its world premiere at the Yale Repertory, where it was a huge success, and soon went on to even greater success on Broadway. But Fugard said he was convinced he had written "too personal a piece" for it to be so well received. Of the dozen and a half plays he'd written by then, "Master Harold" was the most openly autobiographical. He had been forced to write it, he said, because he "needed to come to terms" with an act of racism he had committed as a 10-year-old boy.

"I think that 'round about three years ago I felt myself to be sufficiently distant from that very, very ugly experience to deal with it, without laying a trip on the audience or myself. I wanted to use it in the correct way as the climactic moment in the play. I did not want to exploit it emotionally."

Like the arrogant white boy in the play, which is set on a rainy afternoon in a little rundown tearoom in Port Elizabeth, the South African town where Fugard grew up, the playwright had a strong mother who ran a boarding house café with the help of two black men. Fugard also had a crippled, alcoholic father, toward whom he felt shame and resentment, though rather more love than the title character of the play does.

The racist incident occurred one day after Fugard and

one of the black men, Sam Semela, had closed the café. Fugard rode up to Semela on his bicycle, called his name, and spat in his face. Semela, who had shared Fugard's books and was indeed a spiritual father to him, wiped his face and looked back at the young Fugard with a pity that seared the boy's conscience.

Fugard said he was still at a loss to explain what his motive had been. The event is somewhat changed in the play, as is Master Harold's age, but the guilt that swept over Fugard had remained the same.

"There's a line in 'Master Harold' when the young white boy and this glorious black man are discussing the state of the world," Fugard recalled. "The white boy, agreeing with Sam, says *I know, Sam, I often os-killate* — he mispronounces the word 'oscillate' — *I os-killate between hope and despair as well.* And that statement is as true of me as it is of the character in the play. The pendulum keeps swinging."

The phone began crackling with static. We waited it out. "There are days back in South Africa when the news makes me despair of anything like a nonviolent resolution," Fugard continued. "Well, nonviolent is now out of the question — speedy, let's say speedy resolution of the situation so that at last society will start moving toward decency. We've totally exhausted the patience, the unbelievable patience and forbearance and tolerance of the majority of black South Africans. And I think they rightly see the only recourse to remedy the situation as being violent."

Such views and his longtime collaboration with black actors of the Serpent Players, a small company he founded in 1965, had made Fugard a target of the repressive regime in his native country. He hadn't been jailed, but his associates had been. His telephone was often tapped, he said, and his mail opened. His passport had been confiscated for years at a time.

"At the moment I'm in the for-better-or-worse position where my reputation outside of the country affords me a degree of protection," he said. "In terms of the political climate, I foresee a deterioration back home in the very near future. So I think I may find myself with traveling problems again, as I have on several occasions."

The South African government would have liked nothing better than to bar his re-entry. But Fugard said he was determined not to allow that to happen, and he continued to travel freely. Following his brief stop in Chicago, he would be heading back to the airport for a flight to Thailand, where he was scheduled to play a small role in the movie "The Killing Fields," then being made by the British producer David Putnam.

When I asked Fugard his opinion of race relations in the United States, he replied, "Man! It's not as easy to identify the enemy here, as it is back home, which makes the struggle vastly more complicated. At home the enemy is immediately identifiable — simply because of the institutionalization of racism. Whereas in America the enemy wears many disguises."

He added, "A black man or a gay or someone in any of the minority groups is actually on the receiving end of a lot of prejudice here. But there are certain profoundly stated concepts that you have in terms of individual liberty. They correspond to the American dream. Whether or not it is practiced, at least you have got a dream. Back home we haven't even got that to start with."

Which was precisely the grim failing that struck the most despairing note in "Master Harold ... and the boys."

Chicago Sun-Times, 1983

The despair, it turned out, was warranted. Apartheid would not be dismantled as official policy until 1992, a decade after the play first appeared, and a nonviolent, let alone "speedy," resolution of de facto racism was shown to be impossible.

Author Note

Photo by Janet Leong

Jan Herman is the author of the biography *A Talent for Trouble*, about the life and Hollywood movies of the director William Wyler. He clerked at City Lights Books in San Francisco, where he was the poet-publisher Lawrence Ferlinghetti's editorial assistant. Subsequently, he was a reporter and columnist at the *Chicago Sun-Times*, *The Daily News* in New York, the *Los Angeles Times*, and *MSNBC.com*, where he was also a senior editor. His writing has been published as well in *Partisan Review*; *The Journal of Film History*; *The New York Times Book Review*; *Chicago Quarterly Review*; *Notes From Underground*; *IT: International Times, The Magazine of Resistance*; *Orte*; *Fabrik Zeitung*; *Maintenant: Dada Journal*. His books include the pamphlet *General Municipal Election* (a multimedia rant); *Cut Up or Shut Up* (co-written with Carl Weissner and Jürgen Ploog); *Second Nights*; *Ticket to New Jersey*; *My Adventures in Fugitive Literature*; *Collateral Damage: The Daily History of a Blog*; and *The Z Collection*. His books of poetry include *Your Obituary Is Waiting*; *All That Would Ever After Not Be Said*; *Small Animals*; and *Shadow Words*. He was born in Brooklyn and lives in Manhattan.

Milton Keynes UK
Ingram Content Group UK Ltd.
UKHW050653280324
440307UK00012B/379